The Love in You...

A unique book to share beautiful, loving affirmations with your child.

written & created by debbi mazor, M.A.

Ages 4-7 and anyone of any age who wants to connect to their loving Self.

Balboa Press books may be ordered through booksellers or by contacting:

Balboa Press
A Division of Hay House
1663 Liberty Drive
Bloomington, IN 47403
www.balboapress.com
1 (877) 407-4847

Because of the dynamic nature of the Internet, any web addresses or links contained in this book may have changed since publication and may no longer be valid. The views expressed in this work are solely those of the author and do not necessarily reflect the views of the publisher, and the publisher hereby disclaims any responsibility for them.

Any people depicted in stock imagery provided by Thinkstock are models, and such images are being used for illustrative purposes only.
Certain stock imagery © Thinkstock.

ISBN: 978-1-5043-4686-3 (sc)
ISBN: 978-1-5043-4687-0 (e)

Library of Congress Control Number: 2015920690

Print information available on the last page.

Balboa Press rev. date: 2/8/2016

BALBOA.
PRESS
A DIVISION OF HAY HOUSE

The amazingness of this book!

why: what:

The essence of this book is to instill and experience Loving-Kindness as a "way of being" with your child! This is supported by both of you reading positive, loving qualities and affirmations in rhyme form.

A child's mind is highly impressionable and in a hypnotic theta brain wave through the age of 7—meaning they are being "conditioned." Reading and hearing these loving messages can lead to a greater sense of Self-love and a positive outlook on the world!

who: how:

Have your child sit to your left and read the **left-hand** side of the page...followed by you reading the **right-hand** side of the page to finish the rhyme and reinforce the affirmation.

Ages 4-7 and anyone of any age who wants to connect to their loving Self! If your child is still too young to read, you may read the left side and have your child repeat after you, or they can just listen and experience the love!

when:

This makes for great bedtime reading because your little one's mind is more open to taking in these beautiful, loving messages when they're relaxed and about to fall asleep. Enjoy!

child   parent

Child/parent participation!

Share life-guiding, loving thoughts and emotions with your child in a unique, fun way!

I love being me!
There's no better way...

I love that
you're you,
each and
every day!

I am kind
to everyone I meet...

I love your kindness, it's just so sweet!

I listen quietly when others speak...

You listen
attentively,
and wisdom
you seek!

parent

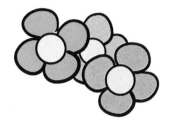

I am always Smiling
my biggest grin...

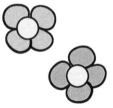

You love to
Smile from ear to chin!

I love helping others, it's what I do...

You are so helpful to all,
and your kindess
shines through!

I am forgiving...
it heals my heart.

child

You are forgiving...
I'd say that's
quite smart!

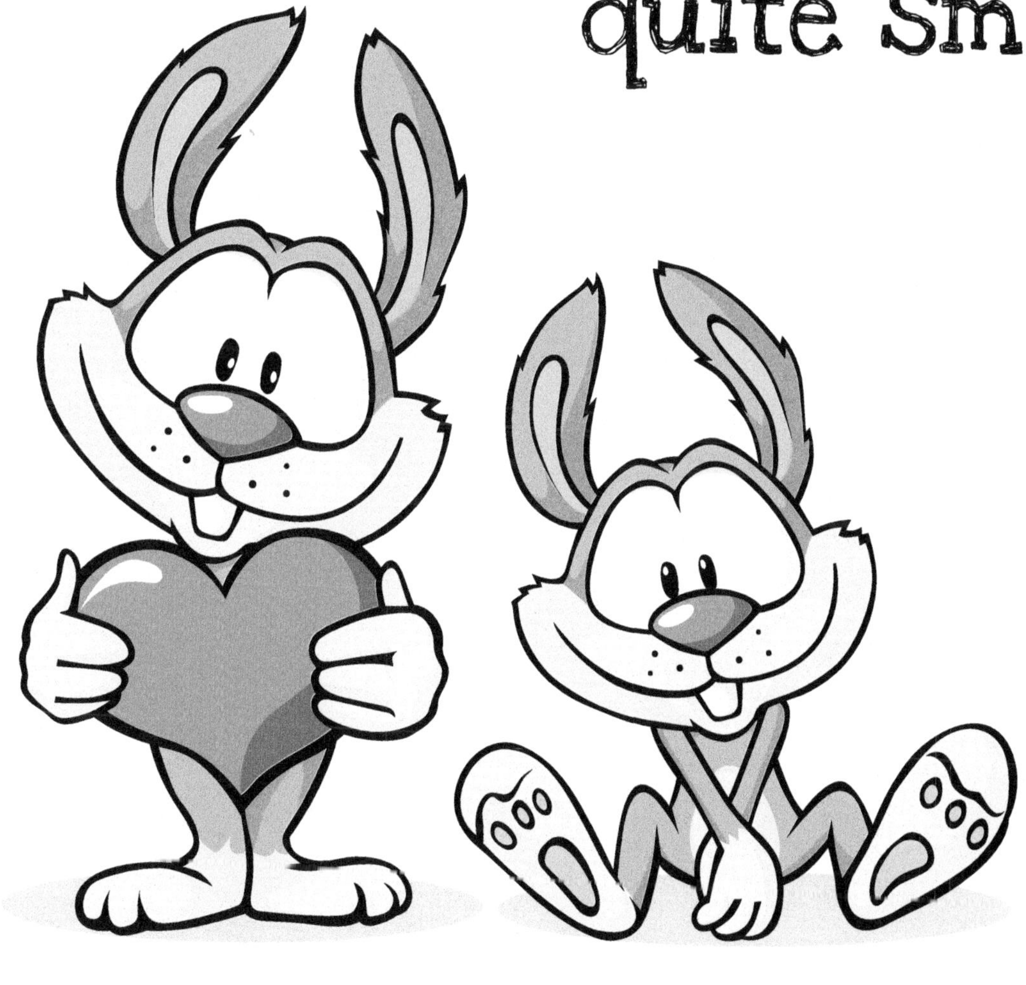

I love to play,
as I'm meant to do...

You love
to play,
& be silly too!

I am so unique...
I LOVE being me!

You are so unique... which the world loves to see!

I am so grateful...
each day I say
THANK YOU!

You are so grateful, and express it with love...TOO!

I follow my heart
in all my choices...

You follow
your heart
and hear all
its voices!

parent

I love everyone... strangers and friends.

You love one and all... your love never ends!

The joy in me,
in you I see...

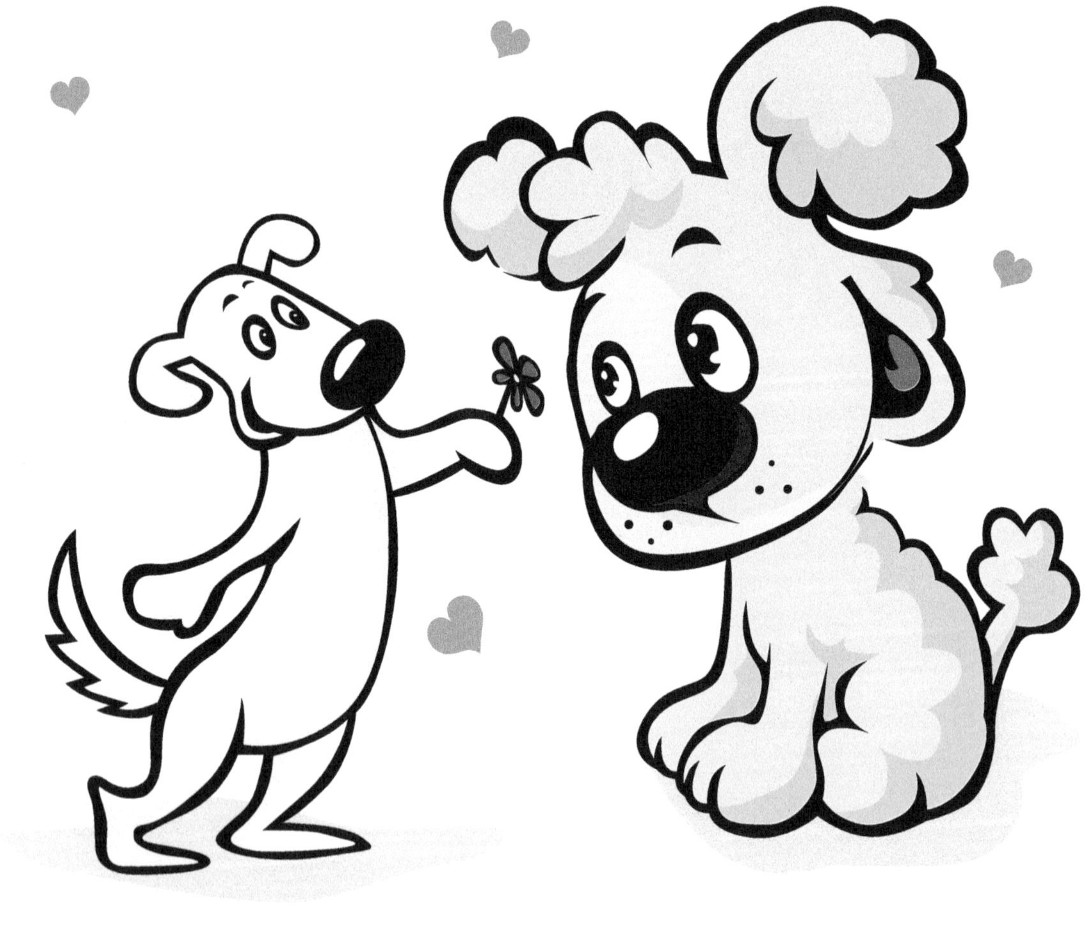

child

In you I see
the joy in me!

parent

I am loving,
I am sweet...

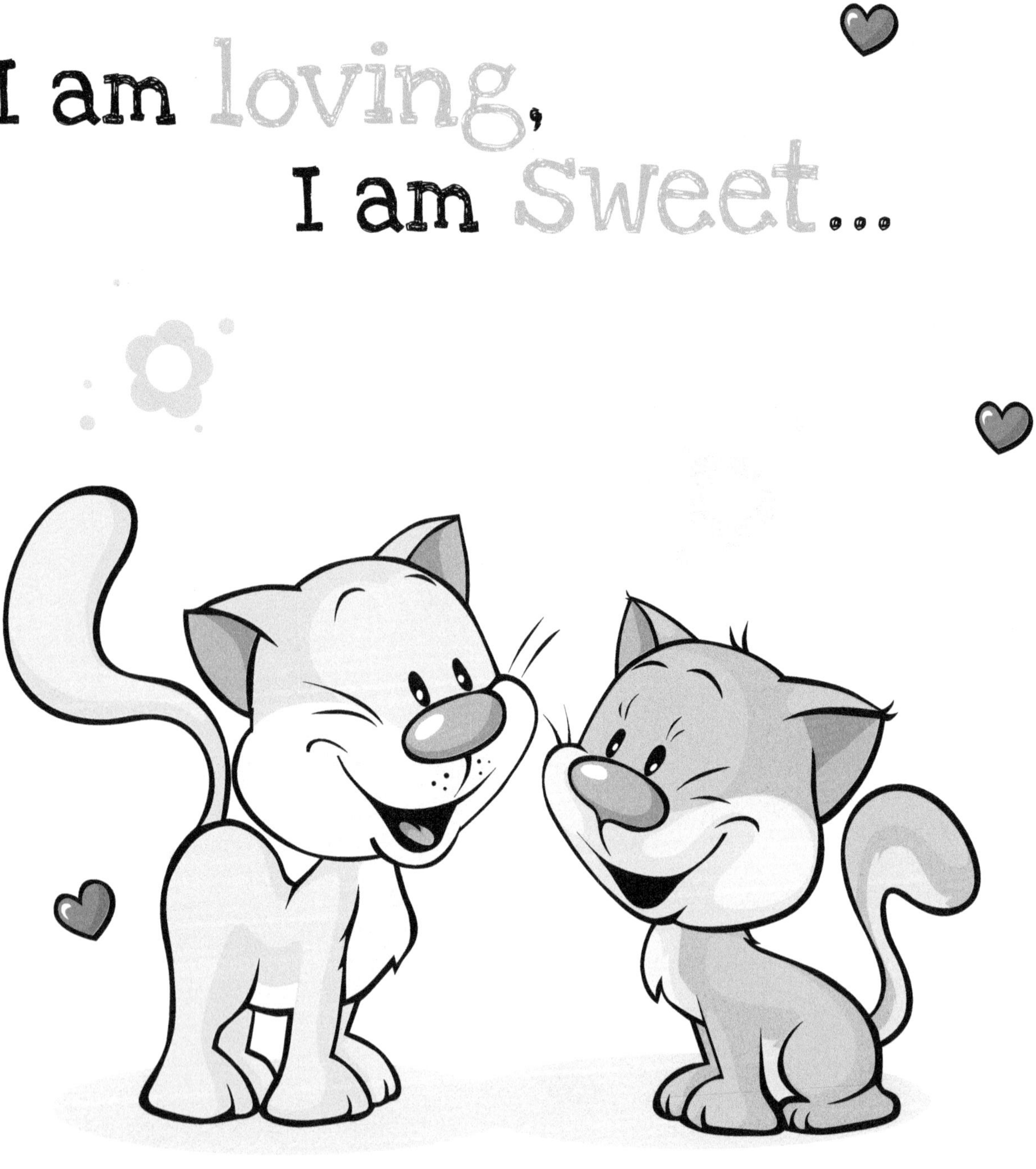

child

You are So
loving & sweet...
OH what a treat!

I am a loving, joyful being!

You ARE your love & joy... I'm Seeing!

parent

I see others as a part of me...

You see the oneness in all, and the love that is FREE!

I am the light and
I shine like a star...

child

You are the light of the world...
...YOU ARE!

See the light and love in the world.

Be the light and love of the world.

Spread your light and love to the world.

about the author:

photo by Kevin McIntyre

Debbi holds a Master's degree in Spiritual Psychology from the University of Santa Monica and loves to assist others with living great lives! Her intention is to create more loving-kindness in the world.

She currently resides in the great city of Chicago and doesn't own a car. As a true city-girl, she loves to walk everywhere!

Follow her blog and sign up for inspirational emails at: debbimazor.com

CPSIA information can be obtained
at www.ICGtesting.com
Printed in the USA
LVOW05s0025230216
476199LV00003BA/3/P